CHARM

*A charm bracelet opens
a magical world of adventure*

Enter the magical world
of the Fairy Realm!

Jessie is living at her grandmother's
rambling old house. She has discovered an
amazing secret – a magical door in her
grandmother's garden leading to a real
fairy world. In the magical Fairy Realm
Jessie meets unicorns and mermaids, pixies
and elves and lots and lots of fairies!

Jessie's magical new friends leave her a lovely
charm bracelet. And each time she visits the
Realm she is given a brand-new charm!

A charm bracelet opens
a magical world of adventure

The Peskie Spell

EMILY RODDA

Catnip
PUBLISHING LTD

CATNIP BOOKS
Published by Catnip Publishing Ltd
Islington Business Centre
3-5 Islington High Street
London N1 9LQ

This edition first published 2007
1 3 5 7 9 10 8 6 4 2

First published in 2006 by the Australian Broadcasting Corporation,
GPO Box 9994 Sydney, NSW 2001

Text copyright © Emily Rodda, 2006

The moral rights of the author have been asserted

A CIP catalogue record for this book is available
from the British Library

ISBN 978-1-84647-018-9

Printed in Poland

www.catnippublishing.co.uk

Contents

CHAPTER ONE

Pesky Weather

It was a fine, sunny Sunday, but a wild wind blew around the old house called Blue Moon, rattling the windows and tossing the branches of the trees. Red and yellow leaves swirled in the air like flocks of small, bright birds.

Inside the house, Jessie glanced up at the leaves flying past the high windows of her grandfather's studio. She felt jumpy and uneasy. She was supposed to be dusting a pile of sketchbooks she'd taken from a glass-fronted cabinet, but she just couldn't concentrate.

'This is what Granny calls "pesky weather,"' she said to her mother, who was sweeping the studio floor. 'Remember that song she always sings when it's sunny and windy both at the same time?'

Rosemary smiled and began to sing, moving her broom in time to the music:

'Pesky weather, nothing goes right!
Pesky weather, lock the Doors tight!
Make a magic brew
With seven drops of dew,
A drop of thistle milk,
And a strand of spider silk . . .'

She broke off, laughing. 'Well, things have gone right for us today, Jess, in spite of the pesky weather,' she said. 'The studio's looking pretty good, now. It'll just need a quick dust before the photographer comes on Thursday.'

'Will Granny be home by then?' Jessie asked. Her grandmother was away seeing some people at the National Gallery who were organising a big exhibition of her late husband's famous fairy paintings. The exhibition was to be held in a few months' time, and a photograph of the Blue Moon studio was going to be part of it.

'Oh, yes,' Rosemary said. 'She'll be back on Tuesday night. How are you going with those sketchbooks, Jess?'

'Nearly finished,' said Jessie hastily. She knew she'd been spending more time looking at the books than cleaning them. The one she was holding now was filled with sketches of trees, leaves, and flowers, and she'd found some real flowers pressed between the pages, too—forget-me-nots, violets, and many other flowers she didn't know.

'Can I borrow this one, Mum?' she asked, holding up the book.

'Sure,' her mother said. 'Just be careful with it. And don't take it outside.'

Jessie put the sketchbook on top of the glass-fronted cabinet and went on dusting the other books and stacking them away.

It was her grandfather's fairy paintings that had made him famous, but he'd painted landscapes, trees, flowers, birds, and animals, too. People who saw his sketchbooks were always fascinated. 'What an imagination Robert Belairs had,' they'd say. 'It's just as if fantasy creatures like griffins and mermaids were just as real to him as lizards and cockatoos!'

Little did they know that there was a very good reason for this—the best reason in the world. Jessie's grandfather had seen griffins and mermaids and other strange beings with his own eyes. He'd seen them in the magical world of the Realm, after he discovered an invisible Door at the bottom of the Blue Moon garden. For years he'd brought back sketches from the Realm. Then, one day, he'd brought back something else: the Realm princess called Jessica, who was to become his wife, Rosemary's mother, and Jessie's very special grandmother.

Only Jessie shared Granny's secret. She'd discovered it by accident and had promised to keep it. She knew she couldn't tell anyone about the Realm. But how she'd have loved to talk about it with her mother, with her best friend, Sal—and even with her school teacher, Ms Stone, who was always criticising her for writing about magical things instead of what Ms Stone called 'real life'!

If only she could tell them about the Realm— and about her friends Giff the elf, Maybelle the miniature horse, Patrice the palace housekeeper, and Queen Helena, who ruled the Realm in her sister Jessica's place! If only she could tell them that every charm on the gold bracelet now jingling softly on her wrist was a gift from the Realm to remind her of an exciting adventure.

The Realm . . .

Jessie frowned. Thoughts of the Realm had brought back the restless, uneasy feeling and now it was stronger than ever.

'Jessie, is something wrong?'

Jessie looked up quickly, meeting her mother's puzzled eyes. 'You've obviously got something on your mind,' Rosemary said. 'Is Ms Stone giving you trouble at school again?'

Jessie forced a smile. 'No,' she said. 'Ms Stone's concentrating on Lisa Wells and Rachel Lew at the moment. She followed them up from the car park on Friday morning and saw that they were jumping over all the cracks in the path. When she asked them why, they said it was because stepping on a crack was bad luck.' Despite herself, she giggled.

Rosemary laughed with her. 'I can just imagine what Ms Stone said about *that*!' she said, turning back to her sweeping.

'Yeah,' said Jessie. 'In class she went on for ages about how stupid it was to believe in things like that. Then she asked everyone to tell her all the sayings about bad luck they knew. She wrote them down and said that on Monday she was going to prove that none of them is true.'

Rosemary shook her head. 'Your Ms Stone's really got a bee in her bonnet about make-believe, hasn't she?' she said. 'It's as if she's on a one-woman quest to stamp it out. She's right about superstitions being silly, of course. But she won't be able to *prove* it. In fact—'

'Yoo-hoo!' called a voice from the back door. 'It's only me.'

Jessie and her mother exchanged rueful glances. 'Come in, Louise,' Rosemary called back. 'We're in the studio.'

Mrs Tweedie, their next-door neighbour, appeared at the studio door. Her spiky grey hair had been blown about by the wind, and her pointed nose was bright red at the tip. Flynn, Granny's big orange cat, was stalking behind her, looking very disapproving.

'I won't disturb you,' said Mrs Tweedie, bustling into the room. 'I just popped in to bring you a few fruit slices I made this morning. They're on the kitchen table.'

'Oh—thank you, Louise,' Rosemary said. 'You are kind.'

It's just an excuse to come in here and poke around, Jessie thought crossly. Then she felt a bit mean. Obviously Mrs Tweedie was lonely. She was avid for details about other peoples' lives because she didn't have any life of her own.

Mrs Tweedie began wandering around the studio, her sharp, bird-like eyes darting everywhere. 'Have you heard from your mother today yet, Rosemary?'

she asked, stopping at the glass-fronted cabinet and beginning to leaf through the sketchbook lying there.

'We won't be hearing from her again till Tuesday,' said Rosemary. 'Her next meeting isn't till then, so she's gone off on a bird-watching camp with some group she met at the gallery.'

'*Really?*' gushed Mrs Tweedie. 'Oh, isn't she *marvellous*.'

'Marvellous,' Rosemary agreed dryly. 'But I wish she'd agree to get a mobile phone. Well, Louise, we'd better—'

'Oh!' squealed Mrs Tweedie, bending over the sketchbook. 'Oh, look what I've found! A pressed flower—*perfectly* preserved! I even caught a whiff of its scent as I turned the page. Jessie, look at this!'

Jessie bit her tongue to stop herself saying that the sketchbook had *dozens* of pressed flowers in it, and that there was no need for Mrs Tweedie to make such a fuss.

But her irritation was replaced by sheer panic when she saw what Mrs Tweedie was looking at. The flower was as delicate as if it were made of fairy wings. Despite its age, its centre was still bright yellow and its petals were a beautiful blue.

Jessie knew without doubt that this was a flower

from the Realm. She'd never seen it before, but there was something about it that breathed magic. How like her grandfather to have put it in the book with perfectly ordinary flowers from the Blue Moon garden! And what bad luck that Mrs Tweedie had seen it!

'What sort of flower do you think it is?' Mrs Tweedie twittered. 'It's *most* unusual.'

'It's just a blue daisy, isn't it?' said Jessie, trying to keep her voice even.

'Oh, I don't think so,' said Mrs Tweedie, putting her head on one side. She whirled around to Rosemary and clasped her hands. 'I know it's a lot to ask,' she said breathlessly, 'but could I borrow this flower for a teeny while? I'd love to try to identify it.'

Jessie held her breath, then felt a wave of relief as her mother looked embarrassed and shook her head. 'I'm awfully sorry, Louise,' Rosemary said, 'but Dad's sketchbooks and all their contents, are—well, rather precious. I don't think it would be right to let anything leave the house—at least while Mum's away. I hope you understand.'

Mrs Tweedie flushed slightly. 'Oh—of course!' she said in rather a high voice. 'Of course. Well. I'd better be going. Don't bother to see me out. I know my way.'

She waved clumsily and hurried from the room. Flynn got up and padded after her, as if he was seeing her off the premises.

'Oh dear! Now I've hurt her feelings,' Rosemary said as the back door slammed.

'You were perfectly right, Mum!' said Jessie vehemently.

Rosemary smiled and shrugged. 'Look, I'll finish up here, Jessie,' she said. 'You go on outside. I know you're dying to get out into the pesky weather, and the fresh air might do you good. Just be indoors by sunset. All right?'

'All right!' Jessie promised gladly.

She took the sketchbook to her room. She pulled on a jacket, and was just about to rush out again when she thought of something. She grabbed an old grey cloak from the top of her wardrobe and stuffed it into her school backpack.

A minute later she was outside, the pack on her back, her long red hair whipping in the wind. She glanced over her shoulder to make sure that Mrs Tweedie wasn't watching over the fence, then ran for the secret garden.

Soon I'll be in the Realm, she thought. Then I'll know. Then I'll know . . .

In the secret garden, the rosemary bushes that

edged the little square of green lawn were as fragrant as ever. The high, clipped hedge still seemed to keep the whole world out.

Jessie gave a sigh of relief. 'Open!' she said. She closed her eyes and waited for the familiar cool, tingling breeze that always swept over her as she moved into the Realm.

But she didn't feel anything at all. And when she opened her eyes she found that nothing had changed. She was still in the secret garden. Jessie blinked in shock.

'Open!' she repeated unsteadily. But again nothing happened. The magic hadn't worked. The Door to the Realm hadn't opened.

She was locked out.

CHAPTER TWO

Maybelle to the Rescue

essie heard a soft, trilling sound behind her and turned quickly. Flynn was sitting in the entrance to the secret garden, watching her gravely.

'The Door's locked, Flynn,' Jessie said. 'Something awful is happening in the Realm, I know it! Oh, if only I could talk to Granny! But she's off bird watching or something, and I can't even ring her!'

She shook her head. 'I've been able to help the Realm before. Maybe I could help this time. But now I can't even try if I can't get in!'

Flynn stood up and stretched. Then he turned around and began walking away, his tail held high.

After a moment, he looked over his shoulder at Jessie. Clearly he expected her to follow him.

Wondering what was in his mind, Jessie let him lead her back up to the house and into the kitchen. To her surprise he didn't stop there, but moved on, into the hallway beyond.

'Where are you going?' Jessie called. But Flynn didn't stop. She hurried after him, and was just in time to see him disappearing into her grandmother's bedroom. Very puzzled now, she followed him.

She found him sitting below the painting that hung on the wall facing Granny's bed. He turned his head toward her and miaowed.

Jessie's eyes widened as she stared at the picture on the wall. Dim and mysterious looking, it showed an archway in a high green hedge, with a blue moon floating in the sky above.

'The secret Door!' Jessie whispered. 'But, Flynn . . . this is Granny's special, private way into the Realm. Do you really think I should—?'

Flynn yawned. It was exactly as if he were saying, 'Do you want to get into the Realm or not?'

Jessie took a deep breath. She moved farther into the room and stood directly in front of the painting. 'Open!' she said in a loud, clear voice.

There was a rush of cold wind. The archway in the painting grew larger and larger, till it was all Jessie could see. She could feel her hair flying around her head. Her skin began to tingle. The sound of wind filled her ears. She screwed her eyes shut as she felt herself being swept away.

After a dizzying moment, she felt soft earth beneath her feet. She waited breathlessly for the wind to die down, for the familiar, sweet sounds of the Realm to reach her ears.

But it didn't happen. The sound of the wind went on and on, mingled with a shrill, chirruping sound that seemed to go right through Jessie's head. And now her skin wasn't just tingling. It was itching unbearably.

What's happening? Jessie thought in confusion. She forced her eyes open and blinked in the bright sunlight.

She was in the Realm. She was standing in front of Queen Helena's palace, on the broad swathe of grass where the Realm folk often gathered.

But nothing looked as it usually did. The trees were tossing in the wind. There were no elves, no fairies, no miniature horses, or palace guards to be seen. The air was thick with whirling shapes that looked like small green leaves. The trembling grass was littered with odd shoes, squashed hats, torn handkerchiefs, and tangled ribbons.

Jessie rubbed her streaming eyes. And then she saw that the green things swirling around her weren't leaves, as she had first thought, but masses of small, flying creatures.

The creatures had hard little wings, thin springy legs, and wild, mischievous, pointed faces like upside-down triangles. Chirruping and clicking, they swooped around Jessie's head, their tiny eyes sparkling like shiny black beads. They were everywhere. The grass and the trees were thick with them. They were swarming all over the palace steps. They were . . .

Jessie screamed as she realised the creatures were swarming all over her, too. Hundreds of them were tickling her, pinching her and tugging at her hair, her clothes and her shoes.

Frantically she tried to brush them off, but it was impossible. Clicking and giggling, the creatures tumbled away under her hands, then darted back instantly to begin their teasing all over again.

Jessie tried to run, and almost at once she tripped and fell. The little green creatures had untied her shoelaces. Gasping, she scrambled to her feet. Then, with a stab of joy, she heard a familiar voice calling her name. She looked up and saw Maybelle galloping toward her through a swirling green cloud. Frayed ribbons hung loose and flapping in Maybelle's tangled mane. Her eyes were wild.

'Maybelle!' Jessie screamed at the top of her voice.

'Jessie, what are you *doing* here?' roared Maybelle, racing up to her. 'No, don't tell me! Let's get out of this! Hold on to me.'

Jessie clutched her friend's mane. Green creatures wriggled out from under her fingers and began bouncing up and down on her hand, flapping their hard little wings and chirruping gleefully.

'Ignore them!' ordered Maybelle. 'Put your head down!'

She began trotting toward the palace. Holding on tightly, her head bent low, Jessie jogged beside her. After a moment the little horse veered to the right and began moving along the side of the palace, toward Patrice's apartment.

As they reached Patrice's door, Jessie noticed a strong smell of oranges. Before she had time to wonder about this, the green creatures clinging to her hands and feet began to squeak and fly away, wrinkling their tiny noses in disgust.

Maybelle kicked the door sharply. 'Patrice!' she bellowed. 'Open up! I've got her!'

There was a scuffling sound behind the door. Maybelle began shaking herself violently. Dozens of green creatures that had been hiding in her mane flew off with a chorus of indignant clicks. 'Brush yourself off, Jessie!' Maybelle shouted. 'Shake your head. Then as soon as the door opens, get in. Fast!'

The door swung open and Jessie bolted through it, with Maybelle hard on her heels. Patrice was waiting for them in her narrow hallway, a large jug of orange juice clutched in her hand. The moment they were safely inside, she slammed the door and stuffed the crack beneath it with an old rug. Then she whirled around to face them.

'Oh, Jessie!' she panted, clutching Jessie's arm. 'How in the Realm did you get here? Oh, what a shock I got when I heard your voice!'

She bustled Jessie into the kitchen, which was filled with the delicious smell of baking. She put the jug of orange juice on the table and pulled out a chair so that Jessie could sit down. 'And I never *would* have heard it, if I hadn't been sprinkling the doormat just at that very moment,' she chattered on. 'Orange juice helps keep them off, you know. For a while. Oh, Jessie, your poor hair—'

'*Her* hair?' Maybelle snorted. 'What about mine? Look at my mane! I'll never get the knots out!'

'Yes, you will,' Patrice said soothingly, bending to peep into the oven. 'I'll help you. But in the meantime, these honey snaps are almost ready. I'll get you both a nice, cool drink, and then—'

'Patrice! Maybelle! What's happening?' Jessie broke in desperately. 'What are those green things?'

'Peskies,' said Maybelle in tones of great disgust. 'They came down from the hills with the wind yesterday, and life's been impossible ever since.'

'*Peskies?*' Jessie gasped, her grandmother's little song suddenly taking on a whole new meaning.

'Here you are, dearie,' said Patrice, giving Jessie a tall glass of lemon drink. 'Just watch out for pips. I've strained it twice, but you never know with Peskies about.'

She put a bowl of lemon drink in front of Maybelle. Then, seeing that Jessie still looked bewildered, she poured a drink for herself and sat down at the table.

'You see, dearie, Peskies mean mischief,' she explained. 'When there are Peskies about, everything that *can* go wrong *does* go wrong. Buttons fall off. Shoelaces break. Things get lost. Milk boils over.

Plates and cups smash. Folk and creatures slip and fall . . .'

'Hair tangles,' grumbled Maybelle. 'Ribbons come loose—'

'Clocks stop,' said Patrice. 'Doorknobs fall off. Chairs collapse. Windows stick. Oh, Jessie, I just can't *begin* to tell you all the trouble Peskies cause.'

'But—there aren't any Peskies in here, are there?' asked Jessie, looking around nervously.

'There could be a few,' Patrice said. 'I've done my best to get rid of them, but they hide, the little wretches. Drink up, Jessie. It will do you good.'

Jessie took a cautious sip of her drink. It was deliciously cool. She began to feel a little better.

'And that's not the worst of it,' Maybelle said soberly. 'Peskies make mischief. But they also eat magic.'

'Eat magic?' Jessie gasped, horrified.

Maybelle nodded. 'They gobble it up,' she said. 'The longer they stay, and the more of them they are, the less magic there is. If we can't stop the plague soon—within a couple of days, I'd say—there'll be no magic left.'

'But can't Queen Helena—?' Jessie began desperately.

She was interrupted by a thunderous knocking at the door and the sound of muffled shrieking.

Patrice leaped to her feet and seized the jug of orange juice. 'Oh, no!' she cried. 'He *hasn't*! He *wouldn't*!'

She rushed out of the kitchen, juice slopping from the jug as she ran. Jessie jumped up and ran after her. She reached the hallway just in time to see Giff the elf tumbling through the front door waving an inside-out green umbrella at the mass of chirruping Peskies swarming in after him.

CHAPTER THREE

A Matter of Memory

'Get out, you little wretches!' screamed Patrice, splashing orange juice at the Peskies. 'Get out!'

The Peskies squeaked and scattered. Most flew out of the door again, but some darted into hiding, so fast that Jessie couldn't see where they had gone. Giff tried to run for the kitchen, slipped on a puddle of orange juice, and fell flat on the floor, wailing miserably.

Jessie ran to help him up. She'd only taken two steps when she felt her own feet sliding out from under her. Screaming, she fell on top of Giff. Patrice slammed the door, whirled around, slipped, and fell over them both. The jug flew high into the air, turning over and over. Orange juice fell like rain.

'Oh, no!' Patrice squealed. She watched in helpless fury as the jug emptied itself and then fell, landing neatly upside down on Giff's head.

'Help!' howled Giff, his voice strangely hollow and echoing. 'Help!' He began struggling wildly. Jessie and Patrice fought to untangle themselves, and at last managed to struggle to their feet. Together they seized the jug and pulled. It came off Giff's head with a loud *pop*, and they all fell backward again.

Watching them from her place of safety by the kitchen door, Maybelle sighed. Then her nose twitched and she looked over her shoulder.

'There's smoke coming out of the oven, Patrice,' she remarked.

'What!' shrieked Patrice. She crawled up and, with Jessie and Giff close behind her, staggered into the kitchen. She hobbled to the stove and tore the oven door open. Black smoke billowed out. Coughing and spluttering, Patrice seized a towel and used it to pull out a tray of what looked like flat, smoking pieces of coal.

'Oh, no!' wailed Giff. 'The honey snaps! They're ruined!'

Patrice dumped the tray into the sink and turned

on the tap. The tray hissed, and more smoke billowed upward. She turned to face her guests. Her hair was dripping with orange juice. Her apron was filthy. She looked furious.

'Giff!' she said in a quiet, dangerous voice. 'Why did you leave your tree house? What *possessed* you to go wandering around in—?'

'I wasn't wandering!' Giff protested, wringing his hands. 'I was coming here, for honey snaps! You said you were going to make some today, Patrice. And I was starving!'

Maybelle snorted. Giff nodded violently.

'I was *starving*!' he exclaimed. 'Last night, I was having a little snack before I went to bed. A Peskie pulled my hair and made me fall off my stool. I fell so hard that I made a hole in the floor. The cookie jar rolled through the hole and fell down to the ground. The cookies all spilled out, and a griffin ate every single one!'

He burst into tears, just thinking about it. Jessie put her arm around him, but Maybelle snorted again.

'You may not have had cookies, but you were *not* starving, Giff!' Patrice said, still in that frighteningly calm voice. 'You had bread and cheese, didn't you? You had fairy-apples. You had—'

'Well—yes.' Giff sobbed. 'But there are some times

when only a cookie will do, Patrice. And all today I just kept thinking, honey snaps, honey snaps, honey snaps, till I just couldn't stand it anymore! So I got out my umbrella, and—'

'*That* umbrella, I presume,' said Maybelle, nodding at the sad mess of spokes and tattered green silk still trailing from Giff's hand. 'Your *new* umbrella. The one *we* gave you for your birthday.'

Giff buried his face in his hands and howled.

'Oh, leave him alone, Maybelle.' Patrice sighed, her anger suddenly dying. 'Giff, it's all right. Stop crying, and I'll see if I can find something nice in the pantry.'

Giff brightened up very quickly at the mention of food. Patrice found a few chocolate chip cookies in a tin, and the four friends gathered around the kitchen table to share them.

'You still haven't told us how you got here, Jessie,' said Maybelle, with her mouth full. 'The first thing Queen Helena did when the Peskie plague started was to lock the Doors. We didn't have time to warn you—it had to be done quickly. Imagine what would happen if Peskies got into your world!'

'I think they do, sometimes,' Jessie said, remembering days at home and at school when nothing seemed to go right.

'Oh, you might have a few, now and then, just like us,' said Patrice. 'But this is different, Jessie. This is a real plague.'

Jessie nodded thoughtfully. 'I came by Granny's secret Door,' she said. 'She's away, but I was worried about you.'

Giff rubbed his cheek against her arm. 'We'll be all right now you're here, Jessie,' he said. 'You'll stop the Peskie plague, I know you will.'

Jessie bit her lip. She didn't see how. 'Can't Queen Helena do anything?' she asked.

Patrice frowned. 'The problem is, Peskies eat magic, so they're very strong. Ordinary banishing spells don't work on them. And it's been so long since the Realm had a Peskie plague that no one knows what to do about it—even Queen Helena. For hundreds of years, a squirt of orange juice has been enough to scare off the few Peskies who were a problem. This plague is another thing altogether.'

'But—but how did it happen?' Jessie stammered. 'I mean—why did the plague start?'

'No one knows,' said Giff. 'It just—happened!'

'Queen Helena is sure there used to be a spell that got rid of Peskies in the old days,' Maybelle put in. 'Not just words—but some sort of brew you made as well.'

'Helena thinks her mother knew it,' Patrice put in. 'She has an idea that there was a rhyme that gave all the ingredients for the brew. But she couldn't find it in the library anywhere.'

Jessie caught her breath. Suddenly her mind was filled with Granny's voice—singing . . .

'Now Helena's gone to see the Furrybears of Brill,' Maybelle was saying. 'The Furrybears know a million old stories. Helena's hoping that the Peskie rhyme might be repeated in one of them. It can't have just disappeared completely.'

'It hasn't!' Jessie heard herself saying, her voice high with excitement. 'It's in the words of an old song Granny sings!'

As her friends listened breathlessly, she began to sing:

'Pesky weather, nothing goes right!
Pesky weather, lock the Doors tight!
Make a magic brew
With seven drops of dew,
A drop of thistle milk,
And a strand of spider silk . . .'

She trailed off, unable to think what came next. 'Try again,' Maybelle urged.

Jessie sang the words again. She could feel the others holding their breath, willing her to go on. But again she stopped. The next line just would not come. She buried her face in her hands.

'You're trying too hard,' said Patrice. 'Just relax for a minute.'

'Are there any more cookies?' Giff asked, looking longingly at the empty plate in front of him.

'No,' Patrice said shortly. 'Make yourself some bread and honey, if you're hungry.'

'You're asking for trouble, Patrice,' muttered Maybelle as Giff scurried eagerly to the pantry. 'There are Peskies about. You've already got orange juice all over the floor. Honey on the ceiling will be the next thing.'

'Oh!' squealed Jessie. She leaped up and her chair tipped backward and fell to the floor with a crash. Maybelle and Patrice jumped. Giff, who was just coming out from the pantry with his arms full, threw up his hands in shock. A loaf of bread and a pot of honey sailed through the air.

'N-o-o!' howled Patrice. Desperately she threw herself forward and caught the honey pot just before it hit the table.

'Good catch!' said Maybelle, then yelled as the loaf of bread hit her on the head and broke in half, covering her with crumbs.

The Peskies who had been hiding under the pantry door giggled wickedly.

'I've got it!' Jessie cried, as if none of this was happening at all. 'Maybelle made me remember!' Excitedly she sang the words:

'Pesky weather, nothing goes right!
Pesky weather, lock the Doors tight!
Make a magic brew
With seven drops of dew,
A drop of thistle milk,
And a strand of spider silk.
Honey is the next thing—one full cup.
Use a stem of rosemary to mix it up.
Add a cup of rain,
Then mix again.
Add a sky-mirror flower,
Soak for half an hour.
Plant the stem straight and true,
Water with the brew,
Say, "Peskies all be gone!"
And your task is done.'

'Dew, thistle milk, spider silk – no problem,' muttered Patrice, writing busily. 'Honey . . . rosemary . . . a cup of rainwater – easy-peasey. It only rains at night, here, Jessie, but it *does* rain. And—?'

'A sky-mirror flower,' said Jessie triumphantly. She saw Patrice look puzzled, and her excitement faded. 'At least, I think that's what the words are,' she added. 'Maybe I heard them wrong.'

'You might have, dearie,' Patrice said slowly. 'I've never heard of a sky-mirror flower. Have you, Maybelle?'

Maybelle shook her head. 'If there is such a thing, it doesn't grow around here,' she said. 'I know every flower within walking distance.' She licked her lips thoughtfully. 'And most of them are delicious, I must say,' she added.

'I've heard of the sky-mirror,' said Giff unexpectedly. 'It's a sort of tree.'

As Jessie, Maybelle, and Patrice stared at him in amazement, he pushed out his bottom lip. 'I do know *some* things, you know,' he said resentfully. 'My mother taught me everything she knew.'

'That wouldn't be much,' Maybelle muttered under her breath. Patrice frowned at her and Maybelle raised her eyebrows innocently.

'So, tell us about sky-mirror trees, Giff,' Jessie said eagerly. 'What do they look like? When do they have their flowers?'

Giff looked uncomfortable. 'Um—I don't know,'

he said, and winced as Maybelle made a rude, huffing sound.

'Never mind,' soothed Patrice, shooting a warning glance at Maybelle. 'Just tell us where in the Realm they grow.'

Giff licked his lips. 'Um—I don't know that, either,' he said.

'What *do* you know about sky-mirror trees, Giff?' Maybelle drawled.

'Um—nothing,' said Giff.

'Told you so,' Maybelle hissed smugly to Patrice. Patrice closed her eyes as if she was praying for patience. Then she opened her eyes again.

'Come on,' she said. 'We're going to tidy ourselves up, then we're going to the palace library. If we can't find a book there to tell us where to find a sky-mirror tree, I'll eat my apron.'

CHAPTER FOUR

The Library

he palace library was a vast, round room inside one of the palace towers. Its curved walls were lined with shelves that stretched all the way from the smooth marble floor to the glass roof high above. Teams of fairies dressed in pale blue were flying rapidly up and down the shelves, taking out books or putting them back in place.

The fairy librarians looked hot and flustered, and Jessie could see why. The library was very busy. The rows of long glass tables in the centre of the floor were piled high with books and crowded with the tall, finely dressed Realm people called the Folk.

The Folk were using their wands to make the

pages of their books turn rapidly. As each book was finished, it was tossed into the air for the fairy librarians to catch and put away. And more books were being added to the tables every minute.

'My word, there'll be some tired wings tonight,' said Patrice, watching one team of tiny fairies struggling upward with a huge red book that wasn't much smaller than Giff.

'Is the library always this crowded?' Jessie whispered.

'Goodness, no!' Patrice whispered back. 'But before she left, Queen Helena asked everyone to keep looking for the Peskie spell, in case the Furry-bears couldn't—'

'We should tell them they can stop now,' squeaked Giff. 'We should tell them that Jessie—'

'Shhh!' scolded a librarian fairy, zooming past his nose. 'Silence in the library! This is your final warning.'

'Unfriendly lot, aren't they?' Maybelle muttered as the fairy darted away.

'They're usually very nice,' said Patrice, looking rather flustered. 'They're just a bit frazzled today, I suppose. Look, let's just do what we came to do. Come on!'

She found a small empty space at the end of one

of the tables, and they squeezed into it, apologising to the Folk on either side of them, who frowned at the disturbance. There was only just room for them all. Patrice and Jessie sat down, Maybelle stood behind them, and Giff sat on Patrice's knee.

Patrice took a slip of pale blue paper from a pile on the table, picked up a silver pencil, and wrote: 'Trees of the Realm.' Then she held the paper up. Almost instantly, a team of fairies swooped down, snatched the paper from her hand, and soared away.

'Now what?' whispered Giff, wriggling impatiently.

'We wait,' Patrice whispered back. 'Sit still!'

In a minute or two the fairies returned, almost hidden beneath a large, thick book. As they put the book down in front of Patrice, Jessie saw that the title was *Trees of the Realm A–Z*. It was very dusty and had a faded painting of a fairy-apple tree in full bloom on the cover. It looked as if no one had opened it for a very long time.

'You look, Jessie,' whispered Patrice, pushing the book over to Jessie. 'You'll be quicker than I will.'

'It's got no pictures inside,' said Giff in disappointment, as Jessie began leafing quickly through the book, looking for trees beginning with S.

'What does that matter?' Maybelle snapped. 'We don't need pictures, we need information.'

'Keep your voices down, for goodness' sake,' hissed Patrice. 'Do you want to get us thrown out?' She sneezed as dust from the book flew up and tickled her nose. 'Bless me,' she murmured and felt for her handkerchief.

Jessie found the *S* section. She started to turn the pages more slowly, running her finger down the paragraphs of small print to make sure she didn't miss what she was looking for.

'Sail Tree . . .' she read under her breath. 'Sausage Tree . . . Seven-Flower Tree . . . Shadow Gum . . . Silent Willow . . . Silver Elm . . .'

Patrice sneezed again. And again. Giff jiggled restlessly. Maybelle snorted, and nudged them both. They turned around to her, whispering crossly.

Trying to ignore them, Jessie turned a page and saw that lying between the next two pages was a piece of broad pink ribbon. Whoever had read this book last had obviously used the ribbon as a bookmark, then forgotten about it. But why was this particular page marked? Could it be . . .?

She felt a little thrill of excitement. Rapidly she ran her eye down the entries on the left-hand page, then pulled the pink ribbon aside so she could begin on the right.

Skallywag Ash . . . she read. *Skinny Oak . . .*

Skipping-Rope Tree . . . Then her heart thudded as she saw the next entry. *Sky-Mirror Tree.*

'It's here!' She gasped.

The whispered argument stopped abruptly. Patrice and Giff swung around and everyone bent to look at the place marked by Jessie's finger. Jessie read with rising excitement:

'Sky-Mirror Tree

The only sky-mirror tree in the Realm grows in the centre of Dally Glade. Its five-petalled, daisylike flowers appear throughout the year. They are very unusual because . . .'

Jessie looked up in surprise as Maybelle, Patrice, and Giff groaned. 'What is it?' she asked.

'We're doomed! Doomed!' wailed Giff. 'Oh, what are we going to do now?' His voice echoed loudly around the enormous room. The reading Folk all raised their heads from their books and frowned.

'Uh-oh,' Maybelle muttered, looking up.

Blue-clad fairies were swooping down on them, shushing them furiously. Jessie snatched her hand away just in time to save it from being flattened as the tree book slammed shut.

'You had your warning,' one of the fairies whispered sternly as the others seized the book and carried it away. 'Please leave at once!'

The four friends had no choice but to do as they were told. They trailed out of the library, not daring to look behind them, but very aware of hundreds of pairs of curious eyes burning into the backs of their necks.

'What's wrong with you all?' Jessie demanded furiously as the library doors closed firmly behind them. 'That was so *embarrassing*! Why did you yell like that? We found out what we wanted to know. The book said that the sky-mirror tree blooms all year, and that it grows in the centre of Dally Glade—'

Maybelle curled her lip. 'Exactly,' she said.

Jessie glanced at Patrice and Giff, who were both looking miserable. 'Oh!' she gasped. 'Don't—don't you know where Dally Glade is?'

'Oh, yes.' Patrice sighed. 'Everyone in the Realm knows about Dally Glade. But it's a problem, Jessie. For a start—'

'For a start it's just about as far away from here as it's possible to be,' Maybelle broke in loudly. 'It's in the west—days and days away, even if we had transport, which we don't. And even if the Peskies would leave us alone while we travelled, which they won't.'

'We're doomed!' Giff whimpered. 'By the time we

get to Dally Glade and back there'll be a million zillion Peskies. And all the magic will be gone!'

'Stop it!' snapped Maybelle. 'Things are bad enough without you wailing and complaining, you fool of an elf! If Dally Glade is where the sky-mirror tree grows, Dally Glade is where we'll have to go. We'll just have to find a way.'

'I won't be able to come with you,' Jessie said reluctantly. 'I promised I'd be home by sunset. But listen, there's something I *can* do to help. I brought Granny's cloak of invisibility with me. You can borrow it for the journey. The Peskies won't see you if you cover yourselves with the cloak, will they?'

'No, they won't,' Patrice said slowly. 'Queen Helena put on her cloak before she left for Brill, and she got away without any trouble. But we've still got to find a way to get to Dally Glade quickly, Jessie. Walking is out of the question. It would take much too long.'

'Wings!' Jessie exclaimed. 'You could borrow some wings and fly there!'

'I don't think wings will work under a cloak, dearie.' Patrice sighed.

'A good thing, too,' muttered Maybelle. 'I look ridiculous in wings.'

'Maybelle, how can you worry about what you

look like at a time like this?' Patrice exploded. 'Sometimes I really wonder—'

'Don't argue!' Jessie cried, holding up her hands pleadingly. 'We haven't got time. We have to think—'

Patrice gasped. Her black button eyes widened. 'Jessie, where did you get that?' she squeaked, pointing at Jessie with a trembling finger.

Bewildered, Jessie looked down and saw that she was still clutching the broad pink ribbon she had found in the library. 'This?' she said blankly, giving it to Patrice. 'Oh—it's nothing. I didn't realise I still had it. It was in the tree book, marking the page where the sky-mirror tree was.'

Patrice smoothed the ribbon between her work-worn fingers. Suddenly her face was shining. 'Oh, Maybelle! Giff! Look!' she whispered.

'I'm looking!' breathed Maybelle. 'And I can't believe my eyes!'

Giff's mouth was opening and closing, but no sound was coming out. He was gaping, fascinated, at the ribbon in Patrice's hand.

'What is it?' Jessie asked, very confused.

'It's a miracle!' Patrice sighed. 'Oh, Jessie, it's our answer! It's our way to Dally Glade. It's a Ribbon Road!'

CHAPTER FIVE

The Ribbon Road

'haven't seen a Ribbon Road for years!' Patrice chattered excitedly as she led the way back to her apartment. 'There were lots of them around at one time, but gradually they were all damaged or wore out. Queen Helena's went years ago—a griffin ate it, as I recall.'

'How does a Ribbon Road work?' Jessie panted, hurrying to keep up.

'You'll see,' said Maybelle. 'Now you can come with us, Jessie. We'll easily be back by sunset. In fact, we've got no choice. No one stays in Dally Glade once the sun goes down. It's forbidden.'

'What I'd like to know is how the Ribbon Road

got into that library book,' Patrice called over her shoulder before Jessie could ask what Maybelle meant. 'Imagine someone just forgetting where they'd left something so valuable!'

'It mightn't have been forgotten,' Jessie said. 'The ribbon was marking the page where the sky-mirror tree was. Maybe one of the Folk wanted to make sure that anyone who had to go to Dally Glade in an emergency would always have a way to get there.'

'I don't think so,' Maybelle snorted. 'The Folk aren't as careful as that. They never prepare for trouble—you can see that by the way they let the Peskie spell get forgotten. "All will be well," they say. And they believe it, too.'

Jessie laughed. Maybelle was right. 'All will be well' was one of her grandmother's favourite sayings. It was one of the things Jessie loved most about Granny, but it often made Rosemary shake her head in despair.

They reached Patrice's apartment and Jessie took the cloak of invisibility from her backpack while Patrice threw a bottle of water and some apples into a small cloth bag.

'Watch out for Peskies,' Maybelle warned. But whether it was because of the strong smell of orange juice, or because the Peskies were just hiding, there were no accidents.

'Now, we'll have to leave by my door because all the other doors in the palace are sealed against the Peskies,' Patrice said, quickly tying the little bag of provisions around her waist. 'And we won't be able to use the Ribbon Road at first. It won't work too close to the palace. We'll hide under Jessie's cloak till we get far enough away. Where do you think we should start the Road off, Maybelle?'

'The safest place would be beside the treasure house, where the griffins are,' Maybelle said, after thinking for a moment. 'The Peskies tend to keep away from there. The griffins ate quite a few of them yesterday.'

Giff moaned. And Jessie felt a knot in her stomach at the thought of facing the fierce griffins—even under a cloak of invisibility.

Giff and Jessie stood on either side of Maybelle, and Patrice stood at the little horse's head and spread the magic cloak over them all. Keeping together, they walked slowly into the hallway and checked in Patrice's long mirror to make sure that they were completely covered.

'I can still see your tail, Maybelle,' said Patrice, her voice muffled beneath the cloak. 'Can you curl it underneath you or something?'

'No, I can't,' said Maybelle crossly. 'The cloak just isn't big enough for all of us. Giff will have to stay here.'

'No,' Patrice said. 'Giff has to come. We need him.'

'*You're* the one who should stay home, Maybelle,' Giff said. 'Dally Glade's no place for a—'

'Don't you tell *me* what to do!' snapped Maybelle.

'It's all right,' Jessie said hurriedly. She tweaked the cloak and managed to arrange it so that even Maybelle's tail was completely invisible.

Cautiously Patrice opened the door and peeped out. The smell of orange juice was still very strong, and there were no Peskies to be seen.

As quietly as they could, the four friends slipped outside and began shuffling toward the back of the palace. They passed the path that led away into the Water Sprites' wood, reached the corner of the palace, and began to move around behind it.

The wind was wild. Bent almost double, Jessie struggled to hold the cloak in place. As it flapped around her, she could see Peskies jumping up and down on the roof of the food storehouse, bouncing on the branches of trees, and swarming all over the flowers.

Some tree branches had already cracked under their weight. Flowers were bruised and crushed. There were several large holes in the storehouse roof, and Jessie could hear bumps, crashes and high-pitched giggles coming from inside.

'Oh, no!' Maybelle groaned softly. 'I hope they haven't got into the oats.'

'Be quiet!' Patrice whispered. 'Do you want them to hear you?'

Painfully slowly, they shuffled on. And then at last Jessie heard the screeching roar of a griffin, and knew that they had nearly reached the treasure house. In one way, she was very relieved. In another way, she was scared to death. She shuddered at the thought of the griffins: four hideous winged beasts that were half lion, half eagle.

They're Queen Helena's pets, she told herself. But this didn't make her feel any better. Queen Helena was far away in Brill, and everyone knew that the griffins didn't obey anyone else.

'Get ready,' she heard Patrice mutter. 'We're nearly there. In a moment I'll unroll the Ribbon Road. Everyone has to put at least one foot on it. We'll have to come out from under the cloak to do that, so be sure to move fast. I'll count three, then everyone say, "Dally Glade." All right?'

'Yes,' Jessie murmured. She felt as if butterflies were flying around in her stomach. She was terrified that somehow she'd do something wrong and be left alone at the treasure house with masses of Peskies on one side and four angry griffins on the other.

'Right. Stop!' said Patrice. Jessie felt the cloak pull tight as the little housekeeper bent to unroll the pink ribbon on the ground. 'Now, everyone step on!' Patrice whispered. 'Quickly, now. One of the griffins is coming to see what we're up to.'

Jessie pulled off the invisibility cloak and looked around wildly. Patrice, Maybelle, and Giff were standing one behind the other, blinking in the light. They all had at least one foot planted on the pink ribbon. Behind them, the end of the ribbon flapped gaily in the breeze.

'Jessie!' wailed Giff. 'Hurry! Get on!'

Jessie tucked the invisibility cloak under her arm and tried to stand on the end of the ribbon. It flapped away from her foot. Desperately she tried again, and managed to stamp on it.

'All right!' she shrieked. The griffin's roars were deafening now. Jessie's hair was blowing around her face so that she could hardly see. But she could see enough to know that the griffin was lunging toward them, its cruel beak gaping wide, and its vast wings spread. She shut her eyes. She couldn't bear to look.

'One-two-three!' gabbled Patrice.

'Dally Glade!' Jessie shouted with everyone else.

And then, suddenly, they were flying—or, not flying, Jessie thought in confusion, but gliding, gliding very fast, as though they were skimming on ice. Wind was beating against her face. She could feel her legs moving, as though she were walking. Yet she wasn't bumping into Giff, who had been standing right in front of her. What was happening?

Fearfully, she opened her eyes. Patrice, Maybelle, and Giff were walking in front of her. They seemed to be walking at a normal speed, yet Giff's hair and Maybelle's mane and tail were streaming behind them, and the woods and meadows on either side of them were rushing past in a blur of green.

Jessie looked down. Beneath her feet was a broad, shining pink band. It was far wider than the little piece of ribbon she had found in the library. It was longer, too—much, much longer—and it was moving. It was stretching ahead into the distance, shining like a stream of fast-running water.

Jessie risked a quick glance over her shoulder. Behind her, the tail of the pink ribbon was curling up and disappearing as it was no longer needed.

She looked ahead again and caught a glimpse of the tip of the Ribbon Road winding up a hill like a snake. And then, in a blink, she herself was rushing up the hill and down the other side, while the Road streaked on toward the west.

'Try to think happy thoughts!' shouted Patrice over the wind. 'It'll help us go faster.'

Jessie did her best. But it was hard to feel lighthearted when there was so much to worry about. What was in store for them in Dally Glade? What if they couldn't find the sky-mirror tree? They didn't even know what it looked like!

And it was hard to relax on the Ribbon Road. She couldn't rid herself of the fear that she'd fall off. Never had she known such speed—not even on an amusement park ride. The feeling was terrifying and wonderful, both at once. Everything was a blur—a blur of speed and rushing sound.

So when at last she felt herself slowing down, and finally stopping, she felt startled and confused, as if she'd just woken from a dream. She blinked around her, only half seeing the shapes of trees and the figures of her friends.

'Everybody off!' she heard Patrice call. 'We're here!'

CHAPTER SIX

In Dally Glade

essie stumbled off the Ribbon Road. Her head was spinning. The ground under her feet seemed to be moving. She heard a high wail and a soft thump beside her.

'Get up, Giff!' she heard Maybelle say. Then she felt Patrice's hand on her arm. 'The giddiness will wear off in a minute, dearie,' Patrice murmured in her ear. 'Just take your time.'

Jessie took a couple of deep breaths. Slowly her head cleared and she could see what was happening around her. Giff was staggering to his feet, groaning and holding his head. Patrice was rolling up a small piece of pink ribbon. Maybelle was standing rigidly still, staring ahead. Jessie turned to see what she was looking at.

It was a huge grove of trees—trees of every shape and kind, rising from a rich green carpet of velvety moss. Some of the trees were tall and straight; some were graceful and spreading. Some had glossy, dark green leaves. Some had leaves so pale that the sun shone through them. Others were a mass of yellow, orange and red.

There was no wind. There were no Peskies, either. The only sound was a strange, soft whispering. The air was tingling with magic.

'What *is* this place?' Jessie whispered. The sun was warm, but she could feel herself shivering. She couldn't tear her eyes away from the mysterious forest. More than anything, she wanted to move into its shade, set her feet upon that soft, green moss, and walk among those whispering trees. And yet she was afraid.

She could see that her friends were uneasy, too. Patrice's hands were trembling as she tucked the pink ribbon away in her pocket. Giff was pale and silent. Even Maybelle was looking nervous.

'One of every kind of tree in the Realm grows in Dally Glade,' Patrice said in a low voice. 'It's a place of safety.'

'It doesn't feel very safe to me,' Jessie murmured.

'I mean it's safe for the trees,' Patrice said, glancing quickly at Maybelle. 'It's very well guarded. We'll have to be careful, and we'll have to be quick. It's getting late. Leave your pack here, Jessie. It's better not to be seen carrying anything. Then they won't think we mean any harm.'

'Who—?' Jessie began. But just then Patrice looked over her shoulder and gave a low cry.

Giff had moved silently away from them and was walking toward the forest.

'Giff, stop! Wait for us!' hissed Patrice, but Giff showed no sign that he had heard her. His eyes were open, but he looked like someone walking in a dream. His hands were tightly clasped. His face was awe-struck.

Jessie, Patrice and Maybelle ran after him and caught up with him just as he stepped into the whispering shade of the first trees. Patrice grabbed his arm, but Giff just kept walking, pulling her along with him. Maybelle gave an angry snort and plunged after them.

Jessie stuffed the cloak of invisibility into her backpack, and dropped the pack on the ground. Then she stepped forward, and the trees closed in around her.

It was like entering another world—a shady, green world that smelled of leaves and sap and growing things. Small pools of golden sunlight dappled the rich moss carpet. Branches made a roof over her head. Soft whispering filled the air.

Maybelle was just disappearing behind a tree with a slender black trunk and heart-shaped red leaves. The tree was like the ones that grew beside the palace treasure house. Her heart pounding, Jessie hurried to catch up. She had no wish to be alone in this strange place. She fell in line behind Maybelle. Ahead she could see Patrice, still holding Giff's arm as he threaded his way through the trees.

On they walked, and on, their feet making no sound on the soft moss carpet. The whispering grew louder, filling Jessie's ears and her mind. Soon she lost track of time. It was hard to remember why she was in the forest at all, and after a while she stopped trying. It was far easier just to walk, drinking in the beauty around her— the whispering trees, no two alike, the carpet of moss, vivid green, dotted with sunlight . . .

And then, in slow surprise, Jessie realised that the pools of golden light had disappeared. Frowning slightly, she looked up. Through the gaps in the leafy canopy above her she saw that the blue of the sky had faded. How did it get so late? she thought dreamily. How long have we been here?

Be indoors by sunset. . . . Her mother's words rushed into her mind like a splash of cold water. And then she remembered another voice— Maybelle's voice. *No one stays in Dally Glade once the sun goes down.*

Jessie felt a stab of fear. She looked ahead and saw the patch of white that was Maybelle moving along a narrow brown track that curved behind a tangle of black branches and red, heart-shaped leaves. Her stomach lurched.

'Maybelle!' she shouted. 'Wait!' She ran forward and touched Maybelle's shoulder. The little horse turned her head slowly. Her eyes were blank. Giff and Patrice had stopped and were looking around, too. Their eyes were as blank as Maybelle's.

'Wake up!' Jessie pleaded, shaking Maybelle violently. 'Giff! Patrice! Maybelle! Wake up!'

Maybelle licked her lips. 'We *are* awake,' she said thickly.

'You're not!' cried Jessie, shaking her again. 'Or not properly, anyway. We've all been walking in some sort of dream. Look!' She pointed to the tree with scarlet leaves and black branches. 'We've been beside this tree before! We saw it at the very beginning, and I think we've passed it a few more times since without realising it. See? We've made a little track in the moss. We've been walking in circles!'

Maybelle's brow creased. She looked at the brown earth beneath her feet and licked her lips again. Then, suddenly, she shivered and shook herself all over. At the same moment, Patrice and Giff gasped and began rubbing their eyes.

'They tricked us,' Patrice mumbled. 'Oh, I thought they'd give us a chance to explain, at least!'

'Who?' shouted Jessie, stamping her foot. '*Who* tricked us?'

'Shhh,' breathed a whispering voice right beside her. 'Sspeak ssoftly, human child.'

Jessie whirled around. At first she couldn't see where the voice had come from. Then her eye caught a movement, and she saw that a strange and beautiful being was sitting on a low branch of the red-leafed tree, right beside her.

The being had smooth black skin, and her slender body was clothed in scarlet silk. Her arms twined gracefully around the slim branches of the tree as if she were part of it. Heart-shaped red leaves were threaded in her long black hair.

Jessie stared in astonishment. Her first thought

was that the being had appeared out of thin air. Then she realised that this wasn't so. It was just that the being looked so like the tree she sat in that if she hadn't spoken and moved, she would have been perfectly disguised.

'Have you been here all along?' Jessie burst out. 'Are you the one who's been leading us in circles?'

'Yesss,' the being answered in a slow, whispering voice. 'I and my ssissters. But now the game is over. The ssun is ssetting, and we musst ssleep. Leave uss, and take the Danger with you.'

'W–what danger?' Jessie stammered, looking wildly around. 'We don't—'

'I think she means me,' said Maybelle flatly. 'She's a dryad, Jessie—a tree fairy. She thinks I'm a danger to trees.'

'You *are* a danger to trees,' Giff quavered. 'You eat leaves, don't you?'

Maybelle tossed her head. 'Occasionally,' she said. She was trying to sound offhand, but Jessie could tell that she was feeling very uncomfortable.

No wonder. The dryad was glaring, and the sound of whispering had suddenly grown very loud.

Jessie looked from side to side, and her eyes widened. Dryads were staring down at them from every tree. Every dryad looked different, because every one was like the tree in which she lived. One had curly brown hair, brown skin and a stiff, shiny green dress that exactly matched her tree's leaves. Another, who was in a spreading tree with soft golden leaves, had creamy white skin, wispy fair hair, and robes of the palest gold. A third, whose small tree was covered in bunches of bright orange berries, wore orange petticoats beneath her green skirt. She had a round, cheery-looking face, but she wasn't smiling now.

'Dryads, please listen!' Patrice begged. 'We mean the trees no harm. We have come here because the Realm is in terrible trouble.' She took Giff's arm and pulled him forward a little. 'As you can see, Giff the elf is one of us,' she went on. 'Surely you know that elves are tree-friends?'

The dryads nodded, but their serious expressions did not change. 'For all we know, you have brought the elf with you by force,' said the one in the red-leafed tree. 'Let him sspeak. We know he will not lie to usss.'

If Patrice felt insulted by these words, she didn't show it. She nodded encouragingly to Giff, who looked as if he might faint with fright.

'Sspeak, ssmall elf!' said the dryad with the curly brown hair.

Giff's ears were drooping almost to his shoulders. He was shaking all over. His mouth opened and closed, but no sound came out.

'Come on, Giff,' Jessie whispered desperately. 'You've got to do this! You're the only one who can help us now.'

CHAPTER SEVEN

Sky-Mirror

Giff made a huge effort to pull himself together. 'Peskies!' he said in a strangled voice.

'Pesskiess!' The dryads leaned forward, their faces troubled.

'Millions of them,' Giff croaked. 'They're eating the magic, hurting the trees, hurting everything. Soon—soon they'll spread here as well. We—we found a spell to make them go away. But to make it we need—we need . . .'

His voice dried up. He gulped.

'We need a flower from the sky-mirror tree,' Jessie burst out, unable to keep silent any longer.

There was a shocked silence. Then the dryad with

the orange petticoats put her head on one side and stared at Jessie. 'Who are you, to sspeak of taking a flower from Dally Glade?' she asked bluntly. 'My tree and I sseem to know you, yet thiss cannot be.'

'This is Jessie, granddaughter of our true queen, Jessica,' Patrice said quickly. 'She looks very like Jessica did when she was young.'

'Ahh,' the dryads breathed. 'Jesssica . . .'

'Do you know my grandmother?' Jessie asked eagerly.

The dryad in the orange petticoats smiled. 'Princesss Jesssica came here many times,' she said. 'She came by a Ribbon Road, as you did. She was a true tree-friend. And sso was the human man she loved. At firsst we ssuspected he was a Danger, as many humans are. But he wanted only to make pictures of uss.'

Jessie nodded, suddenly certain she knew who had left the Ribbon Road in the tree book. It was just the sort of careful, sensible thing her grandfather would have done.

The dryads had begun whispering together. The whispering grew and spread, until it seemed that every tree in Dally Glade was rustling its leaves.

Jessie waited, in a fever of impatience. Blushes of rosy pink were now staining the sky. The sun was setting. She couldn't help thinking about what her mother was going to say to her when she got home.

If I get home, she thought suddenly, looking around at the serious faces of the dryads. What if they decide we're not telling the truth? They might keep us wandering around in this forest forever!

The whispering stopped, and the dryad in the red-leafed tree turned to Giff. 'We have decided to trusst you,' she said. 'Sso we will guide you to Ssky-Mirror. Pesskies are a threat to all of uss, but only Ssky-Mirror can decide to give one of her blooms for the sspell.'

'Come thiss way,' called the fair-haired dryad, beckoning gracefully. 'You musst hurry. No sstranger has ever been in our Glade sso late, sso near to darknesss. Take care the Danger does no harm.'

Very aware that they were being closely watched, Jessie, Giff, Patrice and Maybelle passed the golden tree, then moved on toward the centre of the forest. This time their path was made easy. The moss was springy, and seemed to hurry them along. Branches moved aside to let them pass, and a dryad leaned from every tree, pointing the way.

None of them had any idea what the sky-mirror tree looked like, and yet, the moment they saw it, they all knew it at once. It was smaller than the trees that surrounded it, though its gnarled trunk and spreading branches looked very old. Its soft green leaves were almost hidden beneath masses of beautiful pink daisy flowers. Magic seemed to stream from it, mingled with a delicious perfume that reminded Jessie of orange blossom.

Sitting on a low branch was a sweet-faced dryad with long brown hair. She was watching the strangers' approach intently.

'You and Giff go ahead, Jessie,' Patrice muttered, stopping abruptly. 'Maybelle and I will wait here.'

'Are you afraid I'll lose my head and grab a few sky-mirror leaves for dinner or something?' Maybelle snorted, baring her teeth. 'What do you think I am?'

'It's what the dryad thinks that matters,' Patrice hissed back. 'Stop scowling, Maybelle! Or at least stop showing your teeth!'

Jessie took Giff's hand and led him to the ancient tree. Beneath its canopy, the air had a faint pink glow, and was heavy with the sweet, magical perfume. The dryad sat absolutely still, almost invisible in her bower of pink and green.

Jessie's knees were trembling, and shivers were running up and down her spine. She glanced at Giff and saw that his eyes were filled with awe. She knew that he wouldn't be able to say a word. She took a deep breath.

'Greetings, Sky-Mirror,' she said in a low voice. 'We have come—'

'Shhh, Jesssie,' the dryad whispered. 'There is no need to sspeak. My ssissters have told uss who you are, and what you wishh.' Lovingly, she caressed the flowers above her head with long, slim fingers. Jessie waited, biting her lip.

'My tree and I have sspoken of your quesst,' whispered Sky-Mirror. 'Our flowers are precious to uss. Yet ssometimes we shhed one, as a gift of love to a sspecial friend. Our lasst gift was long ago. And it is longer sstill ssince we gave a bloom for the Pesskie sspell. But we remember. Ah, yess. We remember.'

The leaves of the tree rustled as if stirred by a soft breeze. The dryad stretched out her cupped hand and onto the palm fell one perfect pink bloom. Smiling, she leaned forward and gave the flower to Jessie.

Weak with relief, Jessie stammered her thanks. Then, holding the flower carefully, she backed away from the tree. Tugging Giff's hand to make him follow, she turned and ran back to where Patrice and Maybelle were waiting.

'You did it, Jessie!' said Patrice as she took the flower from Jessie's hand and put it in a silk-lined box she had brought especially for the purpose.

'I did it, too,' said Giff, finding his voice at last.

'Of course you did,' said Patrice, quelling Maybelle's disdainful snort with a sharp look. 'We couldn't have done it without you.'

They followed their own tracks back through the forest, surrounded by the whispered farewells of the dryads who leaned from their trees to watch them pass. At the forest's edge, Patrice unrolled the Ribbon Road once more.

'The return trip won't take long,' she said as everyone stepped on to the shining pink band. 'There'll be no shortage of happy thoughts this time.'

'Yes!' whooped Giff. 'Now you can make the brew, Patrice, and by morning the Peskies will be gone!'

'We still need a stem of rosemary,' Maybelle pointed out, clearly tired of being left out of things. 'There's a big old rosemary bush near the treasure house, I remember. We can get a stem from there.'

'Oh, that old bush died ages ago, Maybelle,' said Patrice. 'But Queen Helena's planted a new bush, right outside the palace kitchens. We'll get what we need from there.'

'Hmff!' snorted Maybelle, and Jessie felt a twinge of sympathy. First the dryads of Dally Glade had regarded the little horse as a menace, and now even her suggestion about the rosemary had proved to be mistaken.

But Giff, Patrice, and Jessie herself were far too happy for Maybelle's injured pride to slow down the Ribbon Road. As Patrice had promised, the return trip seemed to take no time at all. The glorious sunset was only just fading as they reached the treasure house and ran beneath Jessie's cloak to Patrice's apartment.

When they got there, they were surprised to find Queen Helena sitting at the kitchen table with her head in her hands.

'I used the key under the mat, Patrice,' Queen Helena said, after she'd recovered from her own shock at seeing Patrice, Maybelle, Giff, and Jessie suddenly appear from beneath the cloak. 'I just had to rest quietly for a while before I faced the Folk in the palace. I hope you don't mind.'

'Of course not,' exclaimed Patrice. 'It's wonderful you're back, your majesty. We—'

'Oh, Patrice, the Furrybears were no help at all!' Queen Helena broke in despairingly. 'They were so excited they just kept telling me story after story about all sorts of things. I must have heard thousands before I finally got away. But none of them were about the Peskie spell.'

She sighed. 'By the way, there are some Peskies in here, did you know? I found out when I tried to make some hot chocolate. I'll have some more milk sent to you from the palace kitchen. I'm sorry about the milk jug.'

'Queen Helena, it doesn't matter!' Patrice laughed. 'Nothing matters! Everything's going to be all right. We've got the spell, thanks to Jessie.'

Queen Helena blinked in shock, and her beautiful green eyes seemed suddenly to focus on Jessie's smiling face. 'Jessie!' she exclaimed. 'How did you get here? The Doors are locked! And what's all this about the spell?'

'It's a long story.' Jessie grinned. 'Patrice, Giff and Maybelle will tell you all about it. But in the meantime, Queen Helena, could you please magic me home? Right now?'

'Of course,' said Queen Helena, clearly very confused, but beginning to smile. 'Are you ready?'

Jessie grabbed the cloak of invisibility from the floor and stuffed it into her pack. 'Ready!' she said.

'We'll let you know what happens, dearie,' called Patrice. 'We'll send a flower fairy—'

Helena raised her hand. And before Jessie had time to do more than call goodbye to Giff, Patrice and Maybelle, darkness had closed in around her.

When she opened her eyes, she was standing in the secret garden. The first star was glimmering in the grey sky. Late, but not too late, Jessie thought in relief. Thank goodness!

She heard her mother calling her. She shouted an answer and ran for the house. Her mind was so full of exciting memories of her amazing day that she hardly noticed that her legs were stiff and aching. And she didn't hear the tiny chirruping sounds coming from her backpack at all.

CHAPTER EIGHT

The Demonstration

hat night, Jessie lay awake for a long time, hoping for news from the Realm. But no fairy messenger appeared at her window, and finally she fell asleep, to have vivid, troubling dreams of wandering in a forest where the trees had come to life.

She woke exhausted and aching in every muscle. She just couldn't make herself get out of bed. When finally she did, she had no time to do more than throw on the clothes she'd put out the night before, gobble some breakfast, grab her backpack and run.

She arrived at school very out of breath, and made it to her classroom just as Ms Stone was calling the roll. Gratefully she sank into her usual place beside Sal, who grinned broadly, raised her eyebrows, and nodded silently toward the front of the classroom.

Jessie looked, and her jaw dropped. A ladder was leaning against the wall beside the blackboard, which was still covered with the list of superstitions the class had made the previous Friday.

'This morning we're going to finish talking about superstitions,' Ms Stone said crisply, walking to the door. 'Please take out your pens and workbooks, and turn to the notes you made on Friday.'

Ignoring the excited whispering that began the moment she turned her back, she opened the door, looked out, and beckoned.

'I bet she's going to make us all walk under that ladder,' Sal hissed as Jessie bent to get her pen out of her pack.

'Oh, no! She wouldn't!' whispered Lisa Wells in horror.

Jessie was hardly listening. She'd just realised that the cloak of invisibility was still in her pack. She'd forgotten all about it. Hoping that no one would notice, she dug deep beneath the folds of soft fabric, feeling around for her pen case.

Ms Stone ushered in a very small boy holding a very large cat carrier. 'This is Michael Tan from

Year Two,' she announced. 'As you may know, Year Two is having its pet show today. Michael has been very kind and agreed to let his pet help us with our demonstration before the pet show begins.'

Michael Tan nodded briskly and pushed his large spectacles back on his nose. He didn't seem at all over-awed to be the centre of attention. He put the cat carrier on the floor, opened it, and lifted out a fat, sleepy-looking black cat with a stubby tail. The cat didn't so much as twitch its whiskers, but lay draped across Michael's arms, absolutely limp, like a furry cushion with legs.

'Tell us your cat's name, Michael,' said Ms Stone, frowning as the class began to whisper again, and everyone at the back half stood, craning their necks to see.

'Hith name ith Mithster Black,' the boy said, in a high, piercing voice. 'He likes thleeping and food. He'th only got half a tail, becauthe a long time ago Dad mowed the end of it off by mithtake. He'th theventeen yearth old, and Mum thays he'll prob'ly die thoon.'

'Right,' said Ms Stone hurriedly as some of the class tittered. 'Thank you, Michael.'

Jessie's fingers closed around her pen case. As she began to pull it out, she heard something that made the blood rush to her face. It was a soft, chirruping sound. It was horribly familiar. And it was coming from inside her backpack.

Jessie froze, her mind flying back to her last minutes in Patrice's kitchen, to the cloak lying unguarded on the floor. She remembered how she'd pushed the cloak into her pack in a hurry. She hadn't checked it for Peskies. She hadn't dreamed . . .

'Jessie, what are you doing down there?' Sal whispered. 'You're missing everything!'

Jessie jerked out her pen case and bumped the back of her head on the edge of the table. Seeing stars, she fumbled with the zipper on her pack, frantically trying to close it.

The zip stuck halfway. As Jessie struggled with it, two small green creatures with wings hopped gleefully out of the pack, bounced twice on the back of her hand, then leaped off and disappeared beneath the table. With a gasp, Jessie dived after them. But the Peskies had hidden. She couldn't see them anywhere.

'Jessica!' snapped Ms Stone from the front of the room.

Pink-faced and breathing hard, Jessie scrambled from under the table. 'Sorry, Ms Stone,' she mumbled. 'I—I dropped something.'

'Well, just leave it for now,' said Ms Stone sharply. 'It won't run away. Are you ready, Michael?'

The boy nodded, and plumped the cat on the ground. It crouched where it landed, looking even more like a furry cushion than it had before.

'Now,' said Ms Stone. 'On our board we have a list of things that are supposed to cause bad luck. I am going to prove to you, once and for all, that they do not. Sally! Stand up, please.'

The smirk disappeared from Sal's face. She jumped to her feet, and her chair toppled backward and hit the floor with a crash. Lisa Wells screamed.

'That was not bad luck, Lisa,' said Ms Stone icily. 'It was sheer clumsiness.'

It was Peskies, Jessie thought. As she helped Sal pick up the chair, she tried to peer under the table without Ms Stone noticing. She thought she caught a glimpse of green out of the corner of her eye, but when she looked again, it had gone.

'Sally, please read out the items on the board,' Ms Stone said, taking a small green umbrella from her table. 'Stop after each one. I'll tell you when to go on.'

Her eyes wide, struggling to keep her mouth from twitching into a grin again, Sal read. 'It is bad luck to walk on the cracks in the pavement.'

'We have no cracks in the classroom floor,' Ms Stone said, with a small smile. 'But I stepped on every crack in the path on my way up from the car park this morning. I called Isaac to walk with me, and he was my witness. Weren't you, Isaac?'

Everyone turned to look at Zac Janowsky. He went red. 'Yes,' he said loudly. His friends all grinned and nudged one another.

'Go on, Sally,' said Ms Stone.

'It is bad luck to break a mirror,' said Sal. Ms Stone held up a small, cracked mirror, and told them she'd broken it before she left home.

'It is bad luck to walk under a ladder,' read Sal. Her voice quavered slightly as Ms Stone walked through the gap between the ladder and the wall. Ms Stone looked at her and nodded sharply.

'It is bad luck to spill salt, unless you throw a pinch of it over your shoulder afterward,' Sal said. Ms Stone took a container of salt from her pocket.

One of the overhead lights began to ping and flicker. Lisa squeaked and clapped her hand over her mouth. Everyone else started talking and giggling.

'Be quiet!' snapped Ms Stone, frowning. 'Now, this is exactly the sort of silliness I've been talking about! The light was due to fail, so it failed. That's all there is to it.'

Crossly, she twisted the top of the salt container to open it. The container slipped from her hand. It bounced on the floor, the lid flew off, and salt spilled everywhere.

At the same moment, one of the window blinds flew up with a clatter, and a poster fell off the wall.

Over the delighted shouts of the class, Jessie clearly heard the gleeful chirruping of Peskies making mischief. I have to make Ms Stone stop the demonstration, she thought wildly. I have to tell her we should leave the classroom.

But one glance at Ms Stone's face, now blotched with angry red patches, made her realise that she'd be silly even to try.

'Sally, go on,' said Ms Stone through tight lips.

'It is bad luck to open an umbrella in the house,' Sal read. She bit her lip to stop herself from laughing as Ms Stone opened the umbrella and held it over her head.

'And the next,' said Ms Stone grimly,

'It is bad luck if a black cat crosses your path,' said Sal, darting a look at Michael Tan and Mister Black.

'Go ahead, Michael,' said Ms Stone. Michael walked to the wall, so that he and his cat were on opposite sides of the door. Then he turned around and took the lid from a small plastic container. The strong, fishy smell of cat food filled the room. Michael put the open container on the floor in front of him.

'Mithter Black!' he called in his piercing voice. 'Fishies!'

The huge cat stirred. Its nose twitched. It heaved itself up and began to pad rapidly toward Michael.

Holding the green umbrella high, Ms Stone began to walk slowly toward the door. Intent on getting to his snack, Mister Black took no notice of her. He walked right in front of her, and buried his nose in the container.

Quite a few people cheered, and Michael Tan beamed as if his cat had done some amazing trick.

'Settle down, please,' said Ms Stone from the door. She was closing the green umbrella. The red patches on her cheeks and forehead were slowly fading. 'Sally, you can sit down now. And, Michael, you can go back to class. Thank you very much for your help.'

Without ceremony, Michael jerked the plastic box away from Mister Black and stood up. Mister Black made a huffing sound and slowly turned his head from one side to the other, as if wondering where the food had gone.

'That is the stupidest cat!' Sal whispered to Jessie, sinking into her chair. Jessie didn't answer. Cold with horror, she was looking at the Peskie dancing on Michael Tan's right shoe.

CHAPTER NINE

Bad Luck

or homework tonight, I want everyone to write a one-page report on the demonstration you've just seen,' Ms Stone said. 'And I hope—'

She broke off as Zac Janowsky stuck his hand in the air and urgently pumped it up and down. 'Yes?' she asked impatiently.

'Something's crawling on his foot,' said Zac, pointing at Michael Tan.

And at that moment, Mister Black saw the Peskie, too. His fur stood on end. He sprang forward with a yowl, thudding down on Michael's feet with all four paws. Michael rocked backward, lost his balance and sat down abruptly. The container of cat food shot out of his hand and turned upside down, spilling its smelly contents on the floor.

Some people laughed. Some screamed. Jessie saw a green blur zoom toward the back of the room. Mister Black tore after it. It was hard to believe he was the same cat. His eyes were blazing. His fur was so fluffed up that he looked twice his normal size. He made a flying leap onto a table, scattering books and pens everywhere. The kids sitting around the table yelled and jumped up, their chairs crashing behind them.

Mister Black sprang onto the long, low cupboard that stood against the back wall. He raced along it, teeth bared. Clay models, paper masks and books went flying. A vase of flowers toppled and smashed, spraying water everywhere.

Dripping wet, and with a yellow chrysanthemum stuck behind his ear, Mister Black yowled and raced on, heading for the front of the room again.

'Catch him!' shouted Ms Stone, losing her composure at last. She dashed forward and trod in the mound of cat food. Her foot shot out from under her, and she grabbed the blackboard for support. As it crashed to the ground, bringing the screaming Ms Stone down with it, the classroom door flew open.

Mr Morris, the teacher from the class next door,

was standing there, his eyes bulging in amazement. Two tiny streaks of green darted past his ear, circled him three times, then sped out into the corridor, clicking excitedly. Mr. Morris's shirt came untucked, a button fell from his cardigan, and one of the lenses dropped out of his glasses. He blinked in astonishment.

Mister Black ran through the smeared cat food and skidded to a halt. His nose twitched. He sat down and began calmly licking his paws.

Sal and some of the others rushed out to help Ms Stone, but Jessie didn't move. She sat with her hands clasped tightly together, filled with guilt. Ms Stone was absolutely right about superstitions. It was Jessie's fault that the Peskies had escaped and caused havoc.

And now they're loose in the school, Jessie thought, panic stricken. Who knows what trouble they'll cause? I'll have to get back to the Realm as quickly as I can and get some of the magic brew. I'll have to think of an excuse to go home.

But she didn't need an excuse. Ms Stone was taken off to the hospital with a sprained ankle. Her classroom was a disaster area. In the end, the principal called all the class parents, suggesting that, if possible, their children should leave for the day.

'Poor Ms Stone. What a disaster!' Rosemary said when Jessie arrived home. 'I suppose Lisa and Rachel are saying it was all because she walked under a ladder and so on.'

'They are,' said Jessie gloomily. 'It's awful!'

'If she'd had an accident in six months' time, they'd have said the same thing,' Rosemary said absentmindedly, putting down the cookbook she'd been reading when Jessie came in. 'Look, Jessie, I'm just going to run up to the store for a minute. There's a recipe here for little apple cakes that I'd like to try, but it calls for green apples, and I've only got red ones here.'

'Wouldn't red ones do?' Jessie asked.

Her mother shrugged. 'Maybe,' she said. 'But maybe not. You've got to be careful with recipes you've never tried before. Anyway, it's a beautiful day—not a cloud in the sky. I'll be glad to get outdoors for a while. You should make the most of your free day, too, Jess.'

I will, Jessie thought, her mind already on the Realm. As her mother left the house, she hurried to her room. Her heart pounded when she saw a folded piece of blue paper lying on her desk.

Eagerly she snatched up the paper and unfolded it, but as she read the scrawled words, her heart sank.

Jessie—

The spell didn't work. We don't know why. We followed the recipe exactly. More Peskies here every minute. Don't come in again. Too dangerous. Don't worry about us.

P., M., & G.

Jessie slumped down at her desk, shaking her head in bewildered dismay. Why hadn't the Peskie spell worked?

Obviously one of the ingredients was wrong, she thought. But which one? I'm sure I remembered the rhyme properly. I'm positive!

She propped her chin on her hands, and gazed through the window. Her mother was right. It was a glorious day. The rough wind had gone and the sky was a pure, clear blue—as blue as the sky of the Realm. But Jessie didn't feel like going outside. She didn't feel like doing anything at all.

There was a sound from the door. She turned to see Flynn stalking in, his tail held high. He sat down at her feet and looked at her inquiringly.

'I've messed things up, Flynn,' Jessie said miserably. 'But I don't know how!'

The sketchbook she'd taken from her grandfather's studio was still lying on the desk in front of her. Idly she began looking through it, only half seeing the drawings and the leaves and flowers pressed between the pages. Granny's little song was running round and round in her mind.

. . . Add a cup of rain,
Then mix again.
Add a sky-mirror flower,
Soak for half an hour . . .

And at that very moment, she turned a page and caught a faint whiff of a delicious, strangely familiar scent. Jessie blinked, focused, and saw the small blue flower she'd looked at with Mrs Tweedie. She stared at it, frowning in puzzlement.

How strange! The whiff of perfume she'd caught as the page turned had reminded her of the orange-blossom scent of the sky-mirror tree.

'I'm imagining things now, Flynn,' Jessie said. She stared down at the flower in the book. It was the same shape as a sky-mirror bloom—a five-petalled daisy with a golden centre—but there the resemblance ended. The petals of the pressed flower were as blue as the sky outside Jessie's window, while the flowers of the sky-mirror tree had been pink. Jessie knew she'd never forget her first sight of that graceful mass of flowers that seemed to reflect the colour of the sunset sky above—

Sky-mirror!

Jessie gasped and sat bolt upright, gripping the edge of the desk. Suddenly she was remembering the words she'd read about the sky-mirror in *Trees of the Realm A–Z*.

Its five-petalled, daisy-like flowers appear throughout the year. They are very unusual because . . .

She'd been interrupted before she could read on. She'd never found out why sky-mirror flowers were so unusual. Now she thought she knew.

'This *is* a sky-mirror flower,' she whispered. 'Sky-Mirror gave it to my grandfather. It was one of her "gifts of love." And it's blue because—because the sky-mirror does what its name says. Its flowers reflect the sky. When the sky is blue, the flowers are blue. When the sky changes colour, the flowers change, too—to pink, or orange, or grey, or black . . .'

And what had her mother said in the kitchen just now: *You've got to be careful with recipes you've never tried before.*

Gently Jessie picked up the pressed flower. Her heart was beating very fast. Calm down, she told herself. This may not mean anything. The Peskie spell didn't say what colour the sky-mirror bloom had to be when it was used in the brew.

But then the words of the fair-haired dryad were ringing in her ears. *No sstranger has ever been in our Glade sso late, sso near to darknesss . . .*

'The rhyme didn't have to say the colour, Flynn,' she exclaimed. 'Dally Glade is forbidden to strangers once sunset begins. And any sky-mirror flower given during the day would have to be blue! The old Realm Folk who made up the rhyme took that for granted.'

The flower in the book was dry, and very old. Would it still work? There was no way of knowing, but Jessie knew she had to try.

She pulled open her desk drawer, found a little box that had once held paper clips, and put the pressed flower gently inside. Then she tucked the box carefully into her pocket, grabbed her cloak of invisibility from her pack, and ran to her grandmother's room.

Flynn padded after her. He watched gravely as she went to the magic painting. As she put on the cloak, he made a low, growling sound. Jessie glanced at him and bit her lip. 'It'll be all right, Flynn,' she whispered.

But she wasn't so sure. Her hands were trembling

as she pulled the cloak more closely around her. She faced the painting, and thought hard of Patrice's kitchen. 'Open!' she said.

The painting seemed to grow larger. And Jessie felt herself being swept toward it, swept into soft, chill darkness.

CHAPTER TEN

Surprises

essie screwed her eyes shut and tried to keep her mind focused on Patrice's kitchen. That's where I have to go, she thought. Patrice's kitchen. Nowhere else . . .

And then she suddenly realised that she had stopped moving. She was warm again. She could hear voices. And she could smell orange juice!

She opened her eyes cautiously, and with a stab of joy realised that she was where she had wanted to be. Patrice, wearing a red-chequered apron, was grimly squeezing oranges at the kitchen bench. Giff was hunched miserably at the table. Maybelle was pacing around, looking worried and irritable.

None of them glanced in Jessie's direction. She remembered that they couldn't see her, and threw off the cloak.

Giff screamed in shock. Patrice whirled around with a startled cry, sweeping a dozen oranges off the bench. The oranges began rolling all over the floor.

'Jessie!' roared Maybelle, stamping her foot. 'What are you *doing* here? Didn't we tell you—?'

'I had to come,' Jessie broke in. 'Listen!' And, as quickly as she could, she explained everything.

'I don't know if a dried sky-mirror flower works as well as a fresh one,' she finished, pushing the little box into Patrice's hands. 'But it's worth a try, isn't it?'

'It certainly is,' said Patrice, her black button eyes gleaming with new hope. 'Anything's worth a try now.'

She whirled round to the bench and swept the remaining oranges aside with a single movement of her plump arm. 'I've got all the other brew ingredients here,' she said, pointing to the row of jars and bottles at the back of the bench. 'All right. Let's start.'

With Jessie, Giff, and Maybelle clustered around her, she began measuring the brew ingredients into a blue-and-white-striped jug. Seven drops of dew, a drop of thistle milk, a piece of spider's web, a cup of honey . . .

'Pass me a piece of that rosemary, Jessie,' she said tensely.

Jessie passed over a fragrant stem of rosemary and watched as Patrice stirred the thick, golden mixture.

'Add a cup of rain, then mix again,' Maybelle prompted, pressing forward.

'I know, I know,' Patrice said impatiently, pulling the cork from a bottle labelled 'Rainwater' and carefully measuring out a cup of crystal clear liquid. She added the water to the brew and carefully stirred again. Slowly the mixture grew thinner, as the water and honey mixed together.

At last Patrice put the sticky stem carefully to one side. 'Now,' she said. She opened Jessie's little box and took out the sky-mirror flower. It looked very faded and fragile in her brown hand. Jessie crossed her fingers for luck, thought of Ms Stone, and gave a snort of nervous laughter.

Patrice dropped the flower into the golden brew. It lay on the surface, pale, dry, and lifeless.

'It's not going to work,' Giff groaned. 'Look at it! It's dead! Oh, doom!'

'Mix it in, Patrice,' urged Maybelle, nudging

Patrice's shoulder. 'It won't do any good just lying there.'

'No,' Patrice said firmly. 'I'm not going to touch it. The rhyme doesn't say to mix the flower in. It says to let it soak for half an hour, so that's what we'll do.' Ignoring Maybelle's snort of disgust, she turned a half-sized hourglass over. Fine silver sand began running from the top of the hourglass to the bottom.

'All right,' she went on, lifting her chin. 'Now I'm going to clean up this kitchen. You can all help me or not help me, as you like. But no one's to think about the brew again, or talk about it, or touch it, until the half hour's up.'

The little housekeeper's voice was strong, but Jessie could see that her eyes had lost their hopeful glint, and her own heart sank.

The next thirty minutes were the slowest Jessie had ever known. She helped Patrice wash up and put things away. Maybelle paced, lashing her tail. Giff crawled around the floor, picking up oranges, dropping them again, and getting under everyone's feet. They all kept looking at the hourglass. No one spoke.

At last, it was time. 'All right,' said Patrice. 'Let's look.'

The friends crept together to the kitchen bench. At the last moment, Jessie shut her eyes. She couldn't bear to look. Then she heard Giff squeal, Patrice gasp, and Maybelle give a high whinny of joy. She opened her eyes, and her heart leaped.

The sky-mirror flower had completely dissolved. And the mixture in the jug was no longer honey gold, but blue as the sky.

'The first brew didn't change colour, did it Patrice?' squealed Giff, jumping up and down. 'It didn't, did it? Did it?'

'No,' said Patrice, smiling broadly as she poured the blue mixture into a glass bottle and corked the bottle tightly. 'This time we've got the brew right— I'm sure of it. Oh, I think everything's going to be all right.'

And everything *was* all right, though none of them was prepared for what happened when Queen Helena planted the rosemary stem in the rich earth beside the treasure house. Well-wrapped in her cloak of invisibility, with Jessie, Giff, Patrice, and Maybelle huddled close beside her beneath their own cloak, Helena pressed the stem firmly into place. Then she watered it with the blue liquid from Patrice's little glass bottle, and called in a ringing voice, 'Peskies all be gone!'

Alerted by the sound of her voice, Peskies began flying toward her from every direction. The four griffins lumbered forward, growling ferociously, snapping their beaks and spreading their enormous wings. 'Oh, paddywinks and sosslebones!' Jessie heard Patrice mutter.

'Patrice! Get back to the palace,' said Queen Helena urgently. 'All of you—go quickly! I'll hold them off for as long as I can.'

'No! We can't leave you here alone, your majesty!' Giff wailed, twisting to look at the approaching swarm. 'We'll defend you. We'll—'

'Look!' Jessie gasped. 'Look at the rosemary!'

Her eyes were wide with astonishment and wonder. The rosemary stem was growing! One minute it was standing small, straight and lonely in the brown earth. The next minute it was sprouting side branches and increasing in size so fast that in two blinks it had become a sturdy shrub as tall as Giff, and four times as wide.

Blue flowers burst into bloom among the new bush's spiky, dull green leaves. A tingling perfume—

similar to the scent that drifted in the secret garden, but many times stronger, and tinged with the scent of orange blossom—filled the air.

The Peskies stopped in midflight. They hovered uncertainly, wrinkling their tiny noses. Then, suddenly, they shrieked. Thousands of them shriveled up and blew away in the breeze like tiny shreds of dead grass. The rest turned and fled back to the hills, desperate to escape.

And as the breeze caught the magical scent and gently wafted it north, south, east, and west, dark clouds of Peskies rose into the sky from everywhere, and vanished like smoke.

'The old rosemary bush that was here had a scent like this,' Jessie heard Queen Helena murmur. 'Why, it must have been what was keeping the Peskies away for all these years. I was sad when it died, but I had no idea it was so special.'

'We did it!' Giff shrieked. 'We're saved!' He tore off the cloak of invisibility, and began capering wildly around the magic rosemary bush. The largest of the griffins roared angrily and bounded forward.

Queen Helena pulled off her own cloak. Seeing his beloved mistress suddenly appear before him, the griffin stopped, crouched, and wagged its lion's tail. Queen Helena scratched its curved beak affectionately. 'Go back to the treasure house now, Boris,' she said softly. 'There's a good boy.'

The griffin turned obediently and lumbered back to its post.

Folk had begun streaming from the palace, waving, cheering and celebrating. Sounds of joy were rising from the surrounding forests and fields as the people of the Realm gradually realised that the Peskie plague had ended.

'Jessie, you've been wonderful!' Queen Helena said. 'How can we ever thank you?'

'Do you think I could have a little bunch of the special rosemary?' Jessie asked eagerly. 'I'd like to take it to school tomorrow. We've got a bit of a Peskie problem there.'

Queen Helena laughed. 'Of course!' she said. 'And also, we mustn't forget . . .' She lifted her hand, and Jessie's charm bracelet made a tiny, jingling sound. Jessie looked down and saw that a new charm now hung from the gold chain. It was a five-petalled daisy. She beamed.

'Thank you,' she said. 'I'm so glad I could help.'

'Jessie always helps,' cried Giff, throwing his arms around Jessie's waist.

'Yes,' Patrice said fondly. 'I don't know how she does it!'

'I suppose she'd say it was all just a matter of human common sense,' Maybelle teased.

'Not this time,' Jessie smiled, looking down at her bracelet. 'This time it was magic. Pure magic. And a little bit of luck.'